I0621310

Queen Sacrifice (a Saxon short story)

JJ Toner

Published by JJ Toner, 2025.

Queen Sacrifice

A Kommissar Saxon short story by

JJ TONER

First published December 2016
Cover: Anya Kelleye
Smashwords edition
ebook ISBN: 9781908519382
Paperback ISBN: 9781908519931
Copyright 2016 JJ Toner

QUEEN SACRIFICE

Chapter 1

Munich, Friday June 29, 1934

KriminalKommissar Saxon peered at the boy's photograph once more. Johann Grau, the missing youth, had a boyish face with mousey brown hair and traces of acne about the forehead. The first fluffy bloom of a moustache appeared like a shadow on his upper lip. A typical boy of 16 with an impudent half-smile, and yet... There was definitely something about the eyes.

He passed the picture across the desk to his new assistant. "Look closely, Keller. Tell me what you see."

"What am I looking for, Boss?"

"Whatever occurs to you."

Oberassistent Werner Keller looked barely older than the missing boy. His experience to date – messing about in boats with the Water Police – hardly equipped him for the rough and tumble of a city police force, but Saxon was glad to have him. Since the Gestapo takeover of the Munich police force, 9 months earlier, many of their best men had been scattered to the four corners of the country. Good men were hard to come by.

Keller puckered his brow in concentration. "He looks constipated."

"Constipated."

"Either that or there's a turn in his eye."

Keller handed the picture back. Saxon looked at it again. Keller was right. Grau did have a slight astigmatism in his left eye, but even allowing for that, there was still something... "Well spotted, Keller. Is that all you can see?"

"His smile is a bit creepy, Boss. It's a wide-eyed look of false innocence. The *who-me* look. You see it when someone farts in the wheelhouse. I've met smugglers on the Rhine with more genuine smiles on their faces."

Saxon laughed. "You think Johann Grau might be a constipated smuggler?"

"Maybe not, Boss, but I think he has something to hide."

Saxon flipped through the file. "We should start with his father, to get a list of his friends. Find us a car."

Before Keller could reach the door, it burst open. Kriminalrat Glasser, the walking skeleton, strode in.

"Leave us, Keller." Glasser waved a bony hand, as if swatting a fly, and Keller scurried out, closing the door behind him.

Glasser sat in the vacant seat. "What are you working on, Saxon?"

Saxon ground his teeth. Barely 6 months earlier Glasser was a lowly Kriminaloberassistent, calling Saxon "Boss", but, since his promotion, their roles were reversed.

Saxon handed the photograph across his desk. The superfluous question put him on his guard. They had discussed the case 12 hours earlier, when Glasser had stressed its importance, not just to the boy's parents, but to the SS and by extension to the Third Reich.

"Ah yes, the missing schoolboy. You haven't found him yet, I suppose?"

"I've only been on the case for a couple of hours. I had to clear my desk."

"You need to be less defensive, Saxon. No one's questioning your abilities or your dedication to your work. What else are you working on?"

Saxon's file cabinet was full to bursting. Painted gunmetal grey, it had the lopsided look of a sinking battleship. He rattled off the litany of his caseload: 5 possible suicides, 17 probable murders, 33 burglaries and countless reports of assault in the streets.

New cases poured in every day. Everyone was working crazy hours, but there was little that the Munich police could do to stem the flow. The list of unsolved crimes kept mounting. The dogs in the streets knew that Ernst Röhm's Brownshirts were responsible for most of these crimes, but they had effective immunity from the law.

Saxon steeled himself for the next onslaught, some new case to add to the ever-growing pile, no doubt. Since the Gestapo takeover of the Munich police, and the appointment of *SA-Obergruppenführer* August Schneidhuber as the new Chief of Police, everything had changed. Priorities changed daily, driven by political imperatives that were as unpredictable as they were imponderable.

Glasser leaned forward, baring his teeth in a ghastly rictus. "Tell me, when did you last take time off?"

Saxon took a moment to recover from the shock before responding with a short snort of derision. "When was the last time any of us had time off?" If this was the opening gambit in some twisted game, he couldn't guess its purpose.

"I'd like you to take a day's leave. I'm acutely aware that you have had no time for your wife and your young son – how old is he now? When was the last time you had a break?"

Saxon sat bolt upright, his mind racing, seeking out the hidden threat behind the unprecedented offer. "It was over a year ago, when the boy was born. He's 17 months old."

"Seventeen months! How time flies! What was the boy's name again? And how is your wife?"

"The boy's name is Samuel. My wife is well. They are both well, thank you."

"Take the rest of day. I don't want to see you back here before Monday."

#

Saxon headed home on foot in the midday sun. Confronted by a phalanx of marching Brownshirts, he stood to attention and gave the odious Hitler salute. To do otherwise would have invited a beating.

When he got home, he found Ruth rocking Baby Samuel on her shoulder. "What do you mean? Don't you have any cases to work on?"

"I've never been busier."

"So why are you here?" Samuel was whimpering. "Hush, little one."

"I told you, Glasser gave me the day. What's the matter with Samuel?"

"And you let that pipsqueak order you around? He has new teeth coming through. We need to give him something to chew."

"He may be a pipsqueak, my love, but he's a senior pipsqueak."

Saxon went to the closet and removed the transverse belt from his old uniform. He handed it to Ruth, and she gave it to Samuel. The baby sank his gums into the belt and peace was restored.

"Glasser's my boss now, Ruth. When he tells me to take a day, I take a day."

"Well, I don't like it. I don't trust Glasser, or Chief Schneidhuber, or any Gestapo. They're scheming something, mark my words."

#

Baby Samuel was quiet most of that night, but Saxon got little sleep. The sounds of Brownshirts rampaging in the streets outside kept him awake. He sat by an open window, smoking, and watched the glow from fires in the city centre.

The next day was Saturday, June 30. Saxon, Ruth and baby Samuel took a tram to the Munich zoo in Hellabrunn Tierpark. The sun shone on streets littered with broken glass and teams of municipal workers with handcarts, clearing up.

The zoo was crowded – one of the few remaining places in the city where people could take their children in relative safety. Samuel laughed at the monkeys and clapped his hands at the rock-hopper penguins, but the old elephant frightened him. He cried, and Saxon bought him a toy giraffe made out of rubber.

By 4:00 pm they were on the return journey, Samuel fast asleep in his father's arms on the tram. He'd had an exhausting day. Approaching their stop on Franz-Nissl-Strasse near the Piperstrasse junction, the tram driver braked suddenly to avoid a convoy of Kubelwagens heading toward the centre of town at speed.

Saxon shifted the child from one shoulder to the other. "The Brownshirts are out in force again this evening."

Ruth shook her head. "They didn't look like Brownshirts to me, dear."

A second glance told Saxon that she was right. The Kubelwagens were full of Gestapo in uniform, all heavily armed. A prickling sensation of anxiety swept over his scalp at the sight. The nocturnal activities of the Brownshirts were bad enough. Armed Gestapo squads would add a toxic element that would make the streets even more hazardous for the ordinary residents of Munich.

The streets were strangely quiet that night. Ruth slept well. Samuel woke twice, and each time Saxon got up to change his diaper and give him a bottle he thought about smoking a cigarette. He had none. There were places where he might buy a packet at such a late hour, but he rejected the idea of leaving the apartment. The streets were not safe at night, not even for an armed police officer, and Ruth objected to his smoking in the apartment, in any case. For some reason, she thought the smoke was bad for Samuel's health.

Saxon fell into a deep sleep in the early hours. The telephone woke him at 7:00 am. Ruth picked it up quickly and handed it to him.

It was Werner Keller. "Sorry to call so early on a Sunday, Boss, but there's been trouble overnight. I thought you would wish to be informed."

#

Saxon walked the two kilometres to the police station in bright sunlight. He marvelled at the city's transformation. There were few people about and the streets, littered with debris 12 hours earlier, were spotless. The scene should have lightened his heart, but there was something sinister about it, some brooding evil lying hidden. Perhaps Keller's words had put him on edge.

A restless, raucous crowd crammed the public area of the police station. Saxon waded past to his office, collecting Keller on the way.

"So, tell me." Saxon opened his desk, found a packet of desiccated cigarettes and took one out. "What have the Brownshirts been up to this time?" He offered a cigarette to his assistant.

Keller declined. "The Führer flew into Munich yesterday morning. He drove straight to the Hotel Hanselbauer where the SS and Gestapo arrested most of the leaders of the Brownshirts. Many have been taken to Stadelheim Prison, some have been shot already."

Saxon froze in the act of lighting his cigarette. "Did I hear you right? The Führer is here in Munich in person, and the Gestapo are carrying out a purge of the Brownshirts?"

"Yes, Boss. He called them all to Munich on some pretext..."

"How many were taken?"

"At least twelve. Some were arrested at the station as they got off their trains and were taken straight to the prison."

"Ernst Röhm?"

"He was the first."

"Do we have a list of names?"

"The desk sergeant has some of the names. Herr Kriminalrat Glasser has the complete list, Boss."

The burning match reached Saxon's fingers. He swore and dropped it into his ashtray. "And where is Glasser now?"

Keller shrugged. "At the prison, I suppose."

#

The desk sergeant wrote out a list of 14 names, adding a note on each one: 'suicide' or 'evading arrest.' One was marked 'heart failure.' Saxon recognized the names of eight senior members of the Brownshirts.

Keller and Saxon slipped out of the police station through the back door, took a car, and headed south to the city morgue.

They found Professor Valachek, the Medical Examiner, hard at work in the inner sanctum, his eyes bloodshot and red-rimmed. He waved a hand at the bodies laid out in the examination room, two to a table. "If you have to slaughter half the population, I wish you'd do it at a civilized hour and stagger the body count a bit. I need my sleep, and I don't have room here for so many."

"Nothing to do with me, Professor." Saxon splayed his palms. "This is the work of the Gestapo."

"Orpo, Schupo, Kripo, Gestapo, it's all the same. All you ever do is create work for me."

Saxon counted 10 bodies. "I thought there were fourteen."

"I've passed four to Hartmann, the undertaker. Some of these will follow in the next couple of hours. I've been told to make room for a lot more."

"What can you tell me about them?"

"They nearly all died by gunshot. Three almost certainly took their own lives. Four were executed – a single bullet to the back of the head from close range. Three were shot in the back."

Keller said, "Attempting to escape?"

"So I'm told."

"The desk sergeant said there was one case of heart failure," said Saxon.

The professor removed the sheet from one of the bodies, a tall, heavy-set middle-aged man. "Wilhelm Berger, an Evangelist pastor. I expect he had a heart attack. I'll know better when I open him up. I'm surprised there was only one. It must have been like a war zone out there last night."

They did the rounds, Valachek peeling back the sheets one by one, while Saxon checked off the names on his list. He paused at one of the faces – a blond-haired boy wearing the uniform of the Hitler Youth.

"What happened to this youngster?"

"Shot in the back of the head." Valachek handed Saxon an identity card. Saxon read the name Stephan Weiss, born 1917.

Chapter 2

They drove to the undertaker's in silence. Hartmann's funeral home was locked and shuttered. Keller hammered on the door until Hartmann opened it. The undertaker was wearing an apron, peeling off a pair of gloves. "Sorry for the delay, Kommissar, I was working on a body in the basement."

Saxon introduced his new assistant. Hartmann shook Keller's hand. "I heard Glasser was promoted. Come through."

He led them to a low temperature room with a high ceiling. Saxon shuddered, not just from the cold. There was something forbidding and final about Hartmann's establishment – even more forbidding and final than Valachek's morgue.

The undertaker switched on a few dim lights and took them on a tour of the four open coffins. Saxon checked off the bodies from his list. Three were of the over-muscular type identified with the Brownshirts. The fourth was a local authority worker from Ulm, called Walter Müller, the year of birth on his identity card, 1883.

In the car on the way back to the police station, Keller clung to the steering wheel like a man on a rollercoaster. "Fourteen bodies, boss! The most I've ever seen in one day was three, when we rammed a smuggler's motorboat in the North Sea."

#

The police station was even more packed with people than before, all clamouring for attention.

Glasser beckoned to Saxon over the heads of the crowd. Saxon slipped through the rabble into Glasser's office and closed the door.

The Kriminalrat's colour was up. "What are you doing back at work?"

"I got a call. I thought I might be needed."

"Didn't I say I didn't want to see you until tomorrow?"

"There are ten dead bodies in the morgue and four more in Hartmann's funeral parlour."

"None of those are your concern, Saxon. What happened this morning was an operation to quell an attempted political coup. The security of the Fatherland was under direct threat from Ernst Röhm and his men. Our orders came direct from the Führer himself."

"So those fourteen murders—"

"—Were all sanctioned by the government. They were all legal killings."

Saxon consulted his list of names. "Walter Müller, a municipal officer from Ulm, Wilhelm Berger, a pastor, and Stephan Weiss, a teenager, certainly too young to be a threat to the government."

"None of your concern. This morning's killings were all political. You heard what happened to August Schneidhuber?"

"No."

"The Führer personally stripped him of his rank and then had him shot by firing squad."

Saxon's legs turned to rubber. He sat down. "Dead?"

"Yes, dead. Of course, dead. Concentrate on the missing schoolboy. That should be your only concern. Now get out of my office."

#

Keller joined the morning traffic, heading west. "Did you get the complete list from him?"

"Schneidhuber has been executed." Saxon's voice was a flat monotone.

Keller looked at him, wide-eyed. "Not our Schneidhuber, our Chief of Police?"

Saxon nodded. "Keep your eyes on the road, Keller."

"God in heaven, what's happening to us, Boss?"

"Apparently, this morning's killings are none of our concern. They were all... political. We must find the missing schoolboy."

The rest of the journey was conducted in silence, an unspoken question hanging in the air. What exactly were 'political' killings, and why couldn't they investigate them? Saxon had never turned his back on a killing before.

The missing schoolboy's father, Tristan Grau, showed them into the front parlour of his house. "You have news of Johann?"

"Nothing yet," said Saxon.

The room was darkened by heavy lace curtains and smelled slightly of damp. A heavy display cabinet occupied one wall. Piles of books, magazines and old newspapers covered the furniture. Grau drew a curtain, throwing a shaft of strong sunlight across the floor. He invited them to sit, sweeping two armchairs clear of magazines and dropping them on the floor. The sunbeam filled with a dancing cloud of dust particles.

Keller lowered his behind onto one of the chairs.

Saxon remained standing. "Have you heard from Johann since you filed the missing person's report, Herr Grau?"

Grau shook his head. "No, nothing." The pain he was feeling was clearly visible in his eyes. "He's never run away from home before. Where do you think he might be?"

"That's what we're attempting to find out. What can you tell us about his friends?"

"He doesn't have many real friends, just boys in his Hitler Youth troop."

"What school does he attend?"

Grau clasped his hands together. "He was in the Luitpold-Gymnasium, but he lost interest in school and left."

Keller said, "You didn't object?"

Saxon directed a frown at his assistant. "When did he leave school, Herr Grau?"

"On the day that Adolf Hitler became Chancellor. The last day of January last year."

"And was that when he joined the Hitler Youth?"

"No. He joined a couple of years earlier, in 1931."

The door crashed open. Keller jumped like a man bitten by a snake.

Frau Grau stumbled into the room, her eyes red from crying, holding a handkerchief to her nose. She sank onto the armchair vacated by Keller. "Shouldn't you be out searching for my son?"

Saxon said, "We need more information to help us find him, Frau Grau. May I ask you, does he have a girlfriend?"

Frau Grau blew her nose noisily on the handkerchief. "Johann's too young for girlfriends."

Saxon and Keller exchanged a quick glance.

Saxon said, "We don't have his identity card. You're sure it's not hidden in his room somewhere?"

"Certain."

"We'd like to check for ourselves."

Herr Grau led them upstairs to his son's bedroom at the back of the house. Keller followed him in.

Saxon held the door open until Grau took the hint and left the room. "Put together a list of Johann's friends and acquaintances, Herr Grau, all right? We'll be down in a few minutes."

Grau hurried down the stairs.

The room was typical of a teenager on the cusp of adulthood. A mahogany wardrobe, a chair, a single bed covered with a child's counterpane. Swastikas and pictures of famous figures from Germany's past covered the walls. The Führer's portrait held pride of place over the door.

Keller pointed to a picture of a Junkers W33 and a balsa wood model of a JU52-3m hanging from the ceiling on a thread. "A budding pilot, I think, Boss."

"Yes, but too young for girls?"

The wardrobe contained the boy's Hitler Youth uniform, newly laundered and pressed. Saxon lifted the mattress and discovered two magazines of the health and fitness variety, their covers featuring muscular young men. Under the magazines, he found a matchbook from a nightclub called 'The Black Flamingo'. He slipped it into his pocket.

Keller stood on the chair to search the wardrobe. He found a pair of boxing gloves and, hidden at the back, a tin box with a hinged lid. It was empty. He showed it to Saxon.

They went back down to the parlour.

Herr Grau handed Saxon a list of names. "I've included every name we could think of. They're all Hitler Youth."

"Thank you."

"If you have any news – any news at all – you can contact me at work. I'm a maintenance worker at the town hall."

"You look after the Rathaus-Glockenspiel?" said Keller.

"Amongst other things – yes."

Frau Grau joined them at the front door. "Please find our son, Kommissar. He's a good boy. He's never been away from the house for more than a day."

"He never goes camping?" said Keller.

"Yes, of course, he goes camping with his troop, but he never goes away on his own. Tell me you'll find him, Kommissar."

She held a hand out toward Saxon. He grasped it in both of his and met her gaze steadily. "We will find him, Frau Grau."

In the car, Keller started the engine. "You're certain we will find him?"

"Certain, but we may not find him alive. Tell me what you thought of Herr Grau and his wife."

"They looked worried, her more than him."

"Don't you think her level of distress was disproportionate? The boy's been missing less than three days."

Keller made no reply, and Saxon interpreted his silence as an admission that the mind of a woman was beyond his comprehension.

Saxon examined the list of names that Grau had given them. He recognized one name straight away. He pulled the list of the 14 bodies from his pocket and confirmed it. "A boy from Grau's troop – Stephan Weiss – is one of the bodies in the morgue."

Keller gave a low whistle.

#

On the way back to the centre of town, they pulled over at a delicatessen and bought a quick lunch. Saxon watched Keller devour enough bratwurst for a family of five. "You were hungry, I think."

Keller wiped his mouth and grinned.

Saxon rang the police station from a telephone box and asked the desk sergeant if there were any messages for him. The sergeant said, "No messages, Kommissar, but hold on, Herr Kriminalrat Glasser would like to speak—"

Saxon disconnected the call.

"Where to next?" said Keller.

"It's late. Drop me back to the station."

#

Glasser was red in the face, fists clenched on his desk. "Did you cut me off on the telephone?"

"I don't think so." Saxon should have inserted a 'sir' here, but he choked on the word.

"Tell me where you've been."

"We went to see young Grau's parents. We have established a positive link between the missing boy and one that died last night."

"What did I say about the names on the Hummingbird list?"

"Hummingbird?"

"The list of legal killings. You are not to trouble yourself about those. Concentrate on the burglaries and find the missing schoolboy."

"Yes, I understand, but Stephan Weiss was a member of Johann Grau's Hitler Youth troop. He was seventeen, far too young to be a Brownshirt."

"You're complicating the case, Kommissar. Organize a search party, find the missing boy."

"And where should we search?"

Glasser's eyes flashed at Saxon. "It's your job to work that out. Get on with it, man."

#

Saxon opened the door to a silent apartment, the strange, unmistakable, glorious smell of infant everywhere. Checking the bedroom, he found Ruth and Samuel both asleep like angels, the boy clutching his toy giraffe. He put a kettle on and prepared a bottle for Samuel. Then he made a cup of coffee and settled into his favourite armchair with Hans Fallada's latest book.

He awoke with a start two hours later, bathed in sweat, the book on the floor, his coffee cold and untouched in the cup.

Chapter 3

They spent the next couple of days visiting the youths on Grau's list, while carefully avoiding the home of Stephan Weiss. As they travelled around the city, they noticed a black car with two occupants watching them. When Keller moved to challenge them, they drove away.

"Gestapo?" said Keller.

"Probably."

On Wednesday, they visited the home of the Hitler Youth troop leader, an old man with a moustache left behind from the time of the Kaiser. He gave them a complete list of youths in the troop – 51 names.

By Friday morning, they had visited 50 of the 51 names.

Keller came into Saxon's office carrying two cups of coffee. He was in high spirits. "I checked Stephan Weiss's address. He lived in the Maisach district."

Saxon sipped his coffee, burning his tongue. "I've told you we've been forbidden from working that case."

"But he was Hitler Youth, nothing to do with the Brownshirts."

Saxon made no response. The expression on his face was enough to signal his disapproval.

"What about the pastor and the municipal officer?"

"All three were legal killings. We can't go near any of them."

"So they expect us to do our job with our hands tied behind us? We have nothing else."

"We have this." Saxon dropped the matchbook on the desk.

Keller picked it up. "The Black Flamingo, in Blumenau. I'm not familiar with it."

"We'll drop in there tomorrow night. Better dress for the occasion."

"What do you suggest, Boss?"

"It's a nightclub. Use your imagination.

#

They met at the top of the staircase leading down to the nightclub. A light mist clung to the ground as the temperature dropped and the heat of the day seeped from the pavements. Saxon had put on an ancient ill-fitting navy twill suit and a striped tie in the national colours. He barely recognized his Oberassistent. Keller had greased his hair, and he was wearing a silk shirt in lurid colours, open to his navel. A medallion hung on a chain around his neck.

"What have you come as?" said Saxon, suppressing a smile.

Keller chuckled. "I was going to ask you the same question, Boss."

"We'll go in separately. Meet me back here in an hour." Saxon checked his watch. Keller did the same.

Keller went in first. Saxon waited five minutes before descending the staircase.

The entrance was guarded by a doorman in a trilby, who placed a light fingertip on Saxon's chest. "This is a private club. Guests must be accompanied by a member."

He looked like a retired boxer, complete with broken nose and foul breath. Saxon smiled at him. "But I am a member. Don't you remember me?" He put a cigarette between his lips and lit it with a match from the matchbook.

The doorman's eyes registered the matchbook. He tipped his hat and opened the door for Saxon. "Have a good evening, sir."

The club reverberated with music with a heavy drumbeat. A bar occupied the centre of the room. Saxon looked around but couldn't see Keller anywhere in the subdued lighting. He took a seat at a vacant table. As his eyes adjusted to the gloom, he found he was overlooking a wooden dance floor the size of a postcard crammed with bodies gyrating in the flickering light of a glitter ball.

He had barely sat down when a waitress approached and offered to get him a drink from the bar. Saxon showed her Johann Grau's photograph. He shouted above the music, "He's a friend. His name's Johann Grau."

She looked at the picture and shook her head. "I can't help you. What can I get you?"

"Nothing, thank you."

"If you take a table, you are obliged to buy a drink."

Saxon ordered a bottle of beer and paid a week's wages for it.

Before the beer had arrived, he was joined at the table by a young man in a sleeveless shirt. "You're new," he shouted.

"Yes, I'm looking for a friend." He showed the picture to the stranger who shook his head and wandered off across the dance floor.

Most of the bodies on the dance floor were male. The few females that Saxon saw had long blond hair and were wearing high heels and pencil skirts. He spotted Keller's oily hair glistening in the light from the spinning glitter ball. Keller gave him a cheesy grin.

The music died, leaving Saxon's ears ringing. Keller headed for the toilets. Saxon followed him as the music started up again. It sounded to Saxon like the same beat, the same song. Mercifully, the sound was muted in the toilets.

Keller was at a basin, stripped to the waist, washing the sweat from his body. "Any luck, Boss?"

Saxon shook his head. "No. You?"

"Yes, I met this girl. She's agreed to meet me when the club closes."

"I'm not interested in your private conquests, Keller. Have you found anyone that knew the boy?"

Keller looked hurt. "This girl. She may have something for us. Leave it with me, sir. You might as well go home to your family."

"We can cover more ground working together."

"Look at yourself, Boss." Keller pointed to Saxon's reflection in the mirror. "They all know what you are."

The figure in the mirror looked older than his years. Every stitch of the suit spelled police. Only the word 'Kripo' stamped on his forehead would have made it more obvious.

Saxon left the club and went looking for a taxi. He couldn't remember the last time the streets of the city were so calm and peaceful.

\#

Saxon arrived home after midnight. Samuel was screaming, Ruth rushing about looking for ways to calm him.

"What's the matter with him?" he said, hanging his jacket on a hook behind the main door.

"Don't leave that there. Put in the wardrobe where it belongs."

Saxon took the jacket into the bedroom. He removed the pants with a sigh of relief and hung the suit in the wardrobe. When he was dressed in his most comfortable clothes he returned to the kitchenette. Ruth was juggling with a screaming infant and preparing a bottle on the stove at the same time.

Saxon took the child from her. "What's he screaming about?" For one moment he thought that the peace in the city was what was upsetting his son. Perhaps Samuel had become accustomed to the sounds of tumult in the streets outside.

"It's his teeth. I gave him your leather belt, but he spat it out."

Saxon bounced the child on his shoulder and the screaming subsided.

Ruth shook her head in amazement. "That child is like two people in one body. You see to the bottle. Give him back to me." She took Samuel from Saxon and placed him on her shoulder. When the screaming resumed, Saxon knew he was in trouble.

\#

On Monday morning, Saxon rose early and walked to the police station in bright sunshine. One week after the purge of the Brownshirts, the transformation was remarkable. Sunday night had been blissfully peaceful, and the streets were clear of debris. No doubt the Führer would take the credit for restoring order. Another great triumph for the Nazi Party. Never mind that they had created the problem in the first place.

The police station was quieter than the morgue, the front desk unmanned. Saxon rang the bell and the duty sergeant emerged from the back room carrying a steaming cup. "Good morning, sir."

Saxon was of a mind to reprimand the man for abandoning his post, but his smile was infectious. "Good morning, sergeant. Anything to report over the weekend?"

"Nothing, sir. That was the quietest weekend I've ever experienced."

Saxon examined the incident log. There were just four entries, all of a trivial nature. A pair of prostitutes brought in for solicitation, two drunken brawls, and a missing cat.

"No burglaries?"

"No, sir."

This was remarkable. The norm had been two or three per night. Surely this was evidence confirming his theory that the Brownshirts were responsible for the burglaries.

Ever eager, Werner Keller was waiting by Saxon's desk.

"Good morning, Keller. By the look of you, I'd guess you have something for me."

"Remember the girl that I met in the club, Boss? Her name's Lottie. She agreed to meet me outside. I waited an hour, but she never came."

"You obviously made an impression there."

"I gave her the station telephone number. She may call me."

"If she does, tell her to meet you at the police station. If she knows anything, she must be interviewed properly."

"Yes, Boss. I'll let you know if she makes contact."

Saxon wasn't optimistic. If the investigation was relying on Keller's magnetic personality, they were in serious trouble.

Keller was still hovering, shifting his weight from one foot to the other.

"Was there something else, Keller?"

"Yes, Boss. I've been thinking about that empty tin box in Johann Grau's bedroom."

"What about it?"

"What do you think it was used for?"

"It looked like a money box to me. But it was empty."

Keller said nothing. Saxon scratched his chin. "Hmm. We'll need to ask his parents about that. In the meantime, get us two coffees. You can help me go through all our burglary cases again. We need a complete list of stolen goods."

Two hours of painstaking police work later, Keller had completed the list of stolen goods. He came bounding into Saxon's office in a state of excitement.

"Boss, Boss, guess what I found."

"Tell me what you found, Keller."

"One of the burglaries on our list was in Maisach, the Weiss household."

"The home of the dead youth, Stephan Weiss?"

"Yes, Boss. That gives us a reason to visit the family."

"But not a reason to investigate the killing."

#

Glasser made an appearance at 10:00 am with a cheesy grin on his gaunt face. "Have you seen what we have in the cells?"

Saxon stiffened. This was a side of Glasser rarely seen these days. It was probably some sort of trap. "The two prostitutes picked up last night?"

"Not them, the other one, Lottie Kleiner." He whistled. "What a beauty!"

Keller jumped from his seat, "Did you say Lottie?"

"Yes, the stunning blonde. Pity about the black eye. Do we know why she was picked up?"

Saxon said, "Keller, check the incident log."

Keller dashed out to the front desk. He returned ten minutes later in a state of barely suppressed excitement. "She didn't have her identity card on her, but it's definitely Lottie, the girl I spoke to at the nightclub on Saturday. She's been beaten. She came in last night of her own volition, looking for protection."

"Take her to interview room one. We'll interrogate her there," said Saxon.

Lottie was dressed in the same tight-fitting party gown she'd been wearing at the club, now creased and twisted about her torso. Her blond hair and heavy tan made an intoxicating mix. Her makeup was in need of attention, and there was a bruise under her left eye. Overall, she had a delicious look of dishevelled vulnerability that seemed to increase her charm.

Saxon sat directly opposite her, Keller to his left. Glasser sat beside her, their elbows touching. Saxon offered her his cigarette packet. She removed one and Keller leant across the table to light it for her.

"You were not carrying your identity card with you last night. You do realize this is an offence?" said Saxon.

"I'm sorry, Herr Kommissar, it's difficult to keep up with all the new laws."

Glasser frowned at Saxon. "My name is Glasser, Kriminalrat Glasser, Fräulein Kleiner. These are my men, Saxon and Keller. The identity card is a minor matter. You're free to leave, but we'd like to ask you a few questions before you go."

She nodded. Saxon asked if she'd like a glass of water. She nodded again, and Keller left the room to fetch it.

Glasser began the interview. "Tell us what happened to you last night, Fräulein. How did you get that injury?"

"I was attacked by a man in the street on my way home."

"The brute." Glasser looked horrified. "He struck you on the face?"

"Yes, but I fought him off."

"Give us his name and we'll arrest him immediately, Fräulein."

"I don't know his name. Please call me Lottie."

"He didn't... molest you, Lottie?" Glasser broke eye contact.

"No. It was nothing, really. As I said, I fought him off. I can look after myself."

Saxon lit a cigarette. "What can you tell us about Johann Grau? You know him?"

"Yes, we are good friends."

"When did you see him last?"

"About a week ago, on the Speichersee. We enjoy boating in the fine weather."

Keller came back. He placed a glass tumbler of water on the table and she took a sip.

"Are you lovers?" said Saxon.

She looked horrified. "No, Kommissar, Johann's only fifteen."

Glasser frowned at Saxon again. "So Lottie, how did you come to spend the night here, in the cells?"

"I had a feeling that my attacker was not alone." She took a deep drag on the cigarette and crossed her legs. "I came in for protection."

"Do you wish to file an assault report?"

"No, no. I'd like to leave now. I have some sleep to catch up on."

"Very well," said Glasser. "If you have any further trouble you know where to find us."

"Keller will escort Fräulein Kleiner to her home," said Saxon.

"Yes, of course," said Glasser.

"You are too kind, gentlemen." She smiled at Glasser, while dropping her cigarette on the floor and grinding it with her high-heeled shoe.

Keller left with Lottie.

Saxon went to the front desk to examine the incident log. The shift had changed. The new desk sergeant said, "Looks like last night was a quiet one, Kommissar."

The incident log contained Lottie Kleiner's name, address and date of birth. She had been admitted to the cells following a drunken fight in the street and an altercation with the desk sergeant.

"Looks like it," said Saxon.

The sergeant laughed. "Even the missing cat turned out to be a false alarm."

#

When Keller arrived back in the station, he was breathless with excitement. "She knows the dead boy, Stephan Weiss."

"Did she have any suggestions as to who might have killed him, or why Grau might have run away from home?"

Keller shook his head. "No, she was shocked to hear about Weiss, and she seemed just as surprised as Grau's parents that Johann was missing. But I gathered there was more to last night's attack than she told us. She was on edge the whole way, and the closer we got to her apartment building the more fidgety she became. And she asked me to walk her to her door."

"She thinks someone is watching her apartment?"

"She wouldn't admit it, but I think so, yes. She knew Pastor Berger too. She was a regular visitor to his church."

"What about the municipal officer, Müller?"

"She didn't know him."

"Is she a member of the Bund?"

"I didn't ask her that, Boss."

"Check their records. And ask the technical people if they can take a set of Lottie's fingerprints from this." Saxon handed Keller a paper bag containing the glass tumbler.

#

Keller quickly established that Lottie Kleiner had never been a member of the *Bund Deutscher Mädel*.

They took a car from the pool and drove back to the Grau house. Herr Grau raised an enquiring eyebrow as he opened the door. Saxon shook his head. "Nothing yet, Herr Grau. We have a couple more questions."

Grau stood back, and they stepped inside. Keller asked permission to visit the boy's room again. Grau waved a hand. "Go ahead."

He took Saxon into the front parlour and offered him a seat.

Saxon remained standing. "Do you know Lottie Kleiner?" he asked.

"The name means nothing to me."

"She's a blonde. She says she's a friend of Johann's. You're sure you don't know her?"

"Certain. As his mother told you, he has no girlfriends. How old is she?"

"Twenty-one."

"A little old for Johann, wouldn't you agree, Kommissar? Has she given you any clues as to where Johann might have gone?"

"No, but she has been helpful. She and Johann were in a boat together on Speichersee on the day he disappeared. Did you know that Johann liked to row on the lake?"

"No, but I taught him to swim in that lake. He loves the place. We took him there often when he was growing up."

Keller came in with the tin box. He placed it on the table and stood back.

Saxon stared at it with furrowed brow. "What can you tell me about this money box, Herr Grau?"

Grau shrugged. "It's Johann's."

"How much did you find in it?"

Grau's hands were clasped like terrified children clinging together. "I don't know what you mean."

"You searched his room when he went missing."

"Yes, of course."

"You found money in this tin box."

"No, no, Kommissar, it was empty, I swear."

Saxon pursed his lips. He glared at Grau. "Why are you lying to us, Herr Grau? Don't you think I can tell a lie when I hear one? Don't you want us to find your son?"

"I'm not lying!" Grau's voice shook.

Keller said, "Should I call Frau Grau, Boss?"

Grau's chin trembled. He slumped onto a chair. "Fifty. There was fifty Marks in the box."

"Fifty."

"Yes, I swear."

"Keller..."

"No, wait, don't call my wife. I'll show you what I found." He opened the display cabinet, took out a porcelain vase and shook the contents onto the table.

Keller counted the money quickly. "3,015 Marks, Boss."

Saxon said, "Is this all you found?"

"Yes. I would never have spent any of it. Whatever he did to earn it, I know it must have been something... something disgusting."

"Like what, Herr Grau?"

"I don't know." Tears streamed down Herr Grau's face.

Chapter 4

Kriminalrat Glasser called Saxon into his office. He had something important to discuss.

"Sit," said Glasser. "Where's Keller?"

Saxon sat down. "He's working on the burglaries. I sent him out with a list of the stolen property."

"What do you think of him? Will he make the grade?"

"I believe so. He has the makings of a good detective."

"Good, good. And how have you been? How's your wife and that boy of yours? Samuel, wasn't it?"

"He's getting his first teeth, but he's well."

Glasser splayed his fingers over a document in front of him on the desk. "I've received this directive from headquarters. The *SS-Hauptamt* in Berlin has ordered the establishment of a number of training centres for SS officers. One of these Junker schools will be set up in the Munich area, and my name has been placed on the list of first intake of students."

"That's excellent news." Saxon meant it. If Glasser were fully occupied in a training camp, Saxon wouldn't have to deal with him.

Glasser showed no signs of pleasure at the prospect. "Yes, well, there are conditions attached to the enrolment. First, I have to complete a written test."

"That should be no problem."

"Second, I have to pass a test of physical fitness."

"Ah."

Glasser raised an eyebrow. "I think that won't be an obstacle."

"Of course not."

"And third, I have to meet a quota."

"A quota?"

"A list of names of undesirables, people who can be deported or sent to the labour camps."

The blood drained from Saxon's face.

"I need ten names. I want you to help me with that."

Saxon took a deep breath. "You want me to give you names..."

"I thought you might know some communists that haven't been rooted out yet, maybe some Jews in hiding. Your wife is Jewish, I'm sure she must have some names."

A hundred ants crawled over Saxon's scalp. The implication was clear: come up with ten names or Ruth and Samuel would be placed on Glasser's list.

#

Keller returned, bubbling with good news. He had found a significant number of stolen items in the possession of a fence called Dieter Peters. "Should we pick him up, Boss?"

"I'm sorry, what did you say?"

"I thought we should pick him up."

"Who?"

"The fence."

"What fence?"

"Are you feeling all right, Boss?"

"Yes, yes. Tell me again."

"Dieter Peters is holding some of the stolen property. I thought we should bring him in for questioning."

Saxon knew the name. Peters was a known criminal, a born thief and low life. He waved an arm. "Pick him up. You really don't need my permission to arrest criminals or bring people in for questioning."

Keller reacted as if he'd been slapped across the face. He stopped at the door. "I drove by the Weiss house in Maisach."

"Didn't I tell you to stay away from the Weiss's?"

"Yes, Boss. I didn't go near them. But Herr Weiss has a new Horch V8 parked outside his house. I wondered what he did for a living, so I asked the neighbours."

"And?"

"He's a common labourer. He works for the railways. That car would have cost him three year's wages."

\#

Peters was a miserable individual. Saxon allowed Keller to conduct the interrogation. Keller did a creditable job. He did everything he could, short of actual physical assault, to intimidate and badger the man into naming those who sold him the stolen property. Peters refused to squeal. His smug smile never left his face. By the end of the session, Keller was sweating; Peters looked cool as an iceberg.

In his mind, Saxon placed Peters at the top of his list of undesirables. If he had to come up with ten names, perhaps they could all be petty criminals like him.

\#

Peace reigned at home. Baby Samuel was sleeping. Ruth was sipping a glass of Hock. She filled a second glass and thrust it at him.

"*Leibling*, I need to talk to you about something," he said.

She shook her head. Her hair was down. "Later. Drink your wine."

"Have you considered visiting your cousin in Austria?"

"No, *Schatzl*, why? Do you want to get rid of me?" She smiled seductively.

Saxon couldn't recall the last time she'd said or done anything remotely seductive. Unfortunately, he found it impossible to respond. His mind was frozen by the word 'quota'. Ruth and the baby were living under a dire threat that she had no knowledge of. He needed to take action to remove them from the threat without alarming her.

"I think you should spend some time in Austria. Take Samuel with you."

"What's this all about, lover? I haven't seen Benjamin in two years."

"Don't you think it's time you did?"

"Drink your wine." She stepped into the bedroom, kicking off her shoes.

"Ruth, I'm serious. I want you to pack a bag tomorrow and take Samuel to Austria. I'm sure your cousin will be delighted to see you."

She appeared in the bedroom doorway, dressed in her slip. "I'll do no such thing. Now come to bed."

\#

On Friday July 13, Glasser called Saxon into his office again. "We've had new orders from Berlin. The Führer made a speech this morning in the Reichstag. He named seventy-seven people who lost their lives on the Night of the Long Knives."

Saxon raised his eyebrows. "The long knives?"

"July first. That's what they're calling it in Prinz-Albrecht Strasse. Of the seventy-seven, he has declared sixty-three legal killings. Eleven have been declared illegal. Of those eleven, just one falls within our bailiwick: the pastor, Wilhelm Berger."

"He died of a heart attack. What about Weiss the youngster, and the municipal office worker from Ulm, Walter Müller?"

"Müller's death has been classified as an accident. The boy is off limits."

Saxon snorted. "Müller was shot in the back of the neck."

"That was unfortunate. He was struck by a stray bullet."

\#

Stephan Weiss's home was in Maisach, a working-class area in the northwest of the city. Approaching the house, Keller pointed out Herr Weiss's new Horch V8 luxury motorcar.

Saxon knocked on the door. "Follow my lead, Keller."

Weiss's father was a slight, mousey individual, with hooded eyes and a Hitler moustache. He invited them inside.

"Frau Weiss is not home?" said Saxon.

"She's gone to Switzerland."

"She has family in Switzerland?"

"Twin sisters in Zurich. She left a couple of days after... On July fourth. I'm not sure she'll ever come back, to be honest."

"Tell me about Stephan. What was he like? What did he like to do?"

"He enjoyed swimming and boxing. He was a good athlete. He had ambitions to qualify for the Olympic boxing team." The weight of Herr Weiss's double loss hit him and dulled the light in his eyes. His head dropped.

"Do you have any idea who might have killed him, or why?"

"No."

"You reported a burglary a week before you lost Stephan. We are here to investigate that."

"You are not looking for Stephan's killer?"

"Not officially," said Saxon.

Herr Weiss exploded. "I don't care about the break in. How can you waste time investigating that while the killers of my son are roaming the streets?"

"You have an idea who killed him?"

"The degenerate sodomites at the club. Corrupting him wasn't enough for them."

"You must understand, Herr Weiss, your son's death has been classified as legal."

"How can the death of my son be 'legal'? He was seventeen."

"He must have got mixed up in the Brownshirts' attempted coup."

"Stephan was never a Brownshirt." Weiss drove a fist down on a tabletop. "He was a member of the Hitler Youth, for God's sake. He idolized the Führer."

"I'm sure you are right, sir. As I said, we are here officially to investigate the burglary, but let me assure you that we will do everything we can to discover why he was killed. Perhaps we could start by taking a look at his room."

The similarities between Stephan's room and Johann Grau's were striking. The same pictures of public figures covered the walls, and whereas Johann preferred model aircraft, Stephan had photographs of Zeppelins. Keller checked under the mattress and found the expected health and fitness magazines. There was no tin box, empty or full. One photograph on the wall showed two youngsters posing toe-to-toe in a boxing ring, dressed in trunks, head guards, and boxing gloves. Saxon took it downstairs and showed it to Weiss.

"One of these is Stephan, I assume? Who's the other boy?"

"Yes, that's Stephan and his friend Johann Grau at the boxing club."

The name of the club, The Graf Spee, was displayed on the wall behind the ring.

#

The Graf Spee boxing academy was located in a better part of the city, not far from the Black Flamingo nightclub.

The first person they met was a janitor with a bucket and mop. Saxon asked to speak to the owner.

"Wait here," said the janitor. He scurried to a room at the back and emerged accompanied by a tall individual with a bald head.

"If you want to join the club, you'll need to talk with the boxing coach, Fritz Franck. He's not in today, but he'll be here tomorrow."

The name Fritz Franck rang serious bells in Saxon's head. Flashing his Kripo identity disk, he ran his eyes over the photographs on the wall and picked out a likely one. "Is this Herr Franck?"

"That's Fritz. That picture was taken on the day the club opened. He's a little chubbier these days."

Franck was a short, stocky type, standing beside an overweight man in clerical garb. "Who's the priest?"

"That's Pastor Berger. He died on the Night of the Long Knives." He shook his head. "They say he died of heart failure."

"You name?"

"I'm Emil Richter."

"Are you the owner of this club?"

"I'm the senior partner. How may I help you, gentlemen?"

"We're looking for this boy." Saxon pulled Grau's photograph from his pocket and showed it to Richter.

"That's young Johann Grau. He's a member of the club. What has he done?"

"Nothing that we are aware of." Saxon put the picture back in his pocket. "When did you last see him?"

"A couple of weeks ago. He was here with his good friend, Stephan Weiss."

"They were close?"

"Yes, they were the best of friends. I haven't seen Stephan for at least a week."

"Is that unusual?"

"Stephan usually comes in every day."

"Stephan's been murdered," said Keller bluntly.

Richter's hand shot to his mouth. He sat heavily on an exercise bench. "God in heaven! That's terrible. Who could have killed Stephan? He was too young to be mixed up in ... anything that would get him killed."

Streaming through the high windows, the early afternoon sunshine fell across a huge picture of Adolf Hitler, and two smaller pictures of the pocket battleship, the Admiral Graf Spee on its launch day – June 30 – the day before the Night of the Long Knives.

Keller examined the pictures. "Who took the photographs?"

"Fritz did. He wangled an invitation to the launch. He has admired the battleship since it first emerged from the drawing board. He even named the club after it." He shook his head. "I still can't believe it. We had hopes that Stephan might qualify for the Olympics."

#

"So, our dead pastor was mixed up with the boxing club," said Keller, as they climbed into the car. "And Franck has an alibi for the night of June 30. What did you think of Emil Richter, Boss?"

"You mean you don't know who he is?"

"No, Boss."

Saxon shook his head in disbelief. "Richter is a major public figure and philanthrope. He contributes to many youth and sports clubs all over Germany."

"A wealthy man, so?"

"Oh yes. He's also a senior member of the SS and a personal friend of the Führer's."

By the time they arrived back at the office, the name of the boxing coach had emerged from the recesses of Saxon's memory. Franck was a petty thief. He'd served time in Landsberg Prison for burglary. He had a brother called Bernhard, also a thief. Saxon told Keller to check the register of SS members for the two brothers.

The search took five minutes. "Fritz Franck is on the register, Boss, but not his brother."

Saxon wasn't surprised. Times had changed. The SS were prepared to enrol all sorts of riff-raff now, to swell their ranks. They'd even taken on Glasser!

"Pull their records. I'd like to see pictures of both brothers. And ask the SS registrar for sight of the fingerprint records for Emil Richter and Fritz Franck."

"Right, Boss."

"Be polite, Keller, and be patient. You know how protective the SS can be of their records."

Keller tried every trick in the book, but he had to admit failure.

"The peacock in charge of registrations in Prinz-Albrecht Strasse wouldn't give me a glass of water if I was dying of thirst."

"Didn't I tell you to be polite and patient?"

"I was, Boss. I was polite. I was patient. But nothing worked."

"You didn't lose your temper?"

"I did, but only after all hope was gone."

#

Saxon briefed Glasser about the boxing club.

"What led you there?"

"Young Grau was an active member. The club coach is an old acquaintance of mine called Fritz Franck."

"I remember Fritz. He had a brother, too. What was he called?"

"Bernhard."

"Before the boxing club, where did you go?"

"We followed a lead that came to nothing."

"At the home of Stephan Weiss."

Finally, Saxon had confirmation that the Gestapo had been watching him.

"That house is on our list of burglaries—"

Glasser's colour deepened. "You disobeyed a direct order."

"As I said, it was on our list of burglaries."

"All right, so you visited a boxing club."

"Yes. We interviewed Emil Richter, the main sponsor."

Glasser snorted. "I never liked that Richter. He throws his money around like confetti. He's from Blumenau, you know, the same as me, but talks like a sainted aristocrat. It's a mystery to me how he ever got into the SS."

"He does a lot of good works."

"He's a slimy turd. He must have bought his way in. You can carry on, Saxon. But I want your word that you won't go near Herr Weiss again."

#

Saxon and Ruth strolled through the Nymphenburg palace park enjoying the July sunshine, along with half the population of Munich. It was Sunday afternoon. Baby Samuel was asleep in his pram, his giraffe beside him.

Saxon took charge of the pram. "Have you thought about spending time with your cousin in Austria?"

"Yes, I've thought about it, but it's not a good idea. Samuel needs his father. You've seen how much he loves you."

"He hardly ever sees me."

Ruth linked arms with Saxon. "And yet he's like an angel in your arms."

"You could go for a short time."

"How short?"

"A month. Two, maybe."

"Tell me why you want me to go."

"You've seen the brutality of the Brownshirts."

"The Führer has put a stop to that. He's removed Ernst Röhm and the other Brownshirt leaders."

Saxon placed his hand over hers on his arm. "Who do you think carried out the purge on the Brownshirts?"

"I don't know. The Führer's personal guard?"

"The Schutzstaffel, the dreaded SS."

"Why dreaded?"

"You won't see the SS causing havoc in the streets, Ruth, but they are far more dangerous than the Brownshirts. No one is safe now that they have taken over."

She looked at him sharply. "Are you telling me I'm in danger?"

"Not yet, but I don't know how much longer I can protect you."

"And Samuel?"

"There is a great Nazi storm coming and I don't want you and Samuel to be swept away."

"Now you're scaring me."

"Chancellor Dollfuss has banned the Nazis in Austria. You'll be safe there."

When they got home, they found Keller waiting at the apartment door. "Sorry to disturb your Sunday evening, Boss, but the Schupo have found Johann Grau."

"Alive?"

Keller shook his head. "He washed up on the shore of the Speichersee."

Chapter 5

Johann Grau's body was badly bloated and decomposed.

"Hardly surprising," said Saxon. "The poor guy's been in the water for two weeks."

"More like twenty days," said Keller.

Saxon looked at him. "How can you be so precise?"

"When I was with the Water Police, we pulled lots of bodies from the Rhine."

Professor Valachek ordered the uniformed Schupo to load the body into his ambulance and took it back to the morgue. Saxon and Keller followed in their police car.

"What can you tell us, Professor?" said Saxon.

Valachek tied his apron around his extended belly. "First impressions, a blow to the back of the head rendered him unconscious. He was pushed or fell into the lake. If I find water in his lungs, then he drowned. If not, the blow killed him. I'd say he's been in the water about twenty days."

Saxon glanced at Keller, who kept a straight face. "Since June 27, then. Could it have been an accident?"

"Possibly, if he drowned, but not very likely. He could have fallen and hit his head on a rock, I suppose. The head wound should tell us a lot about what hit him. We need to establish his identity before I open him up. Can you get his people in this evening? I'd like to get started as soon as possible."

Saxon asked for fingerprints from the body. The professor took a full set of prints and handed the card to Keller.

#

Saxon marvelled at how the Medical Examiner had reduced the bloating to the boy's face for Herr and Frau Grau, but the skin was flabby and a ghastly grey. Frau Grau gave one cry and collapsed. Tristan Grau caught her before she hit the floor, and Professor Valachek waved smelling salts under her nose to revive her.

Tristan Grau agreed that the body was that of his son. His calm demeanour suggested that he was in control of his feelings, but a reddening of his ears told Saxon otherwise. He took the grief-stricken father into an empty room, leaving Frau Grau in the tender care of the Medical Examiner.

"I'm sorry for your loss, Herr Grau."

As soon as Keller closed the door, Grau exploded. "Those bastards killed my boy."

"Who are you talking about, Herr Grau? Who did this to your son?"

"He fell into bad company. They turned him to abomination, and then they killed him."

"Can you give me names?"

"I don't know their names."

Keller said quietly, "You knew your son was meeting with these people, but you did nothing?"

Saxon frowned at Keller and shook his head.

Grau wailed like a soul in hell. "I spoke to him. He laughed in my face. I beat him. He laughed even louder. I locked him in his room. He climbed out the window. He risked a broken neck climbing down a drainpipe. What more could I do? I couldn't stop him."

#

On Monday morning, Saxon examined the photographs of Fritz and Bernhard Franck. Fritz was a typical slack-jawed low-life. The picture of Bernhard was 10 years old. At that time, Bernhard was a fresh-faced youngster.

When Keller arrived, Saxon sent him to find Lottie and bring her in. Keller drove to Lottie's apartment and knocked on the door.

"Who's there?"

"It's Oberassistent Keller from the Kripo. We have some questions."

"Can't it wait? I'm not dressed."

"We need you down at the station, Lottie. I'll wait while you get dressed."

It took a while, but it was worth the wait. Lottie looked even better in summer sunshine than she had in the gloom of the nightclub or the artificial light of the police station. Keller gasped when he saw her. He followed her from the apartment to the car and opened the car door for her. At the station, he ushered her into interview room one. Saxon and Glasser joined them.

"Good morning, Lottie," said Glasser. "I have to tell you that we have found the body of your friend, Johann Grau."

She covered her mouth with a hand. "His body? You mean he's dead?"

"I'm sorry to say, so, yes. I need to ask you where you last saw him."

"I told the Kommissar, the last time I saw him was on the Speichersee."

"When was that?" said Saxon.

Her brow furrowed while she thought about that. "It was a Wednesday, about two weeks ago."

"In June? The last Wednesday in June, perhaps?"

"Yes."

"June 27," said Keller.

"Where was he when you last saw him?" said Glasser.

"I left him tying up the boat in the boathouse, at about six in the evening. We had agreed to meet again, but he never turned up."

Saxon handed her a cigarette. "Where?"

"At the Black Flamingo."

Glasser said, "Wasn't he a little young for nightclubs?"

She shrugged. "He liked to dance. Where did you find him?"

"At Speichersee. He washed up on the shore," Keller said. "It looks likely that he was murdered."

"My God! You think I killed him! Is that why I'm here?"

"No, no, Fräulein." Glasser leant across the desk and patted her hand. "I'm sure you didn't kill him, but you may have seen something, someone acting suspiciously, near the lake, perhaps."

She shook her head. "I'm sorry, I saw no one."

#

While Keller drove Lottie back to her apartment, Saxon followed Glasser into his office. "Why are you letting her go? She must be our main suspect for the killing."

"Don't be ridiculous, Saxon. How could a beautiful young thing like that have committed a murder?"

"She admitted she was with Johann Grau on the lake the day he died."

"Find some real evidence." And Glasser dismissed Saxon with a wave of his fingers.

Saxon went back to his office. He called the city morgue on the telephone. "Do you have anything for us, yet, Professor?"

"Indeed I have," the professor replied. "Drop in the next time you're passing."

When Keller returned from dropping Lottie home, he and Saxon drove to the city morgue again. They found Professor Valachek in his office, enjoying a cup of coffee and an apple pastry.

Saxon smiled. "Good day, Professor."

Professor Valachek replied through a mouthful of pastry. "Sit, gentlemen."

He licked his fingers, opened a file on his desk and read from it. "As I suspected, the Grau boy died as a result of a blow to the back of his head. There was no water in his lungs. The shape of the wound suggested a metal implement of some kind – a wrench, perhaps."

"It was definitely murder, then?" said Keller.

"No question about it. It was a crushing blow, delivered with considerable force. Death would have been instantaneous. I found post-mortem rope burn marks on the body, too. I'd say whoever killed him weighed the body down with rocks. The action of the tides and the decomposition process probably worked the body loose."

"Tides? On a reservoir?"

"Why not? The moon's gravity acts on all large bodies of water."

Saxon took a moment to absorb that information. "And what about the pastor, Wilhelm Berger? Was that a heart attack as you suspected?"

"Ah, now that was an interesting case." The professor flipped through the files on his desk. "Here it is. The immediate cause of death was a sudden catastrophic cardiac arrest. There's no question that the pastor had a weak heart, but he might reasonably have expected to live several more years. Unfortunately, the poor man was the victim of a physical assault that hastened his impending heart failure."

"What kind of physical assault?"

"Somebody tried to throttle him. I found bruising around the neck and throat."

The Medical Examiner gave Saxon copies of his autopsy report on the boy and the pastor and they left the morgue.

#

The next stop was the pastor's dwelling, a modest house in a quiet suburb within walking distance of the boxing club. The journey took five minutes.

As they stepped up to the pastor's door, Keller said, "I left the pictures of the Franck brothers on your desk. Did you see them?"

"Yes, thank you, Keller."

"Did you recognize the younger one?"

"Bernhard? Yes, I know the face. Try the knocker, Keller."

"You didn't make the connection?"

"Is this one of your guessing games?"

Keller used the door knocker. "He looks a bit different now that his nose is broken, but Bernhard Franck is now the doorman at the Black Flamingo."

The door was opened by a woman in her middle years. She had been crying.

Keller flashed his badge. "Police, investigating the death of Pastor Berger."

She invited them inside. "I was beginning to wonder if anyone would ever care to find out what happened to Pastor Wilhelm. I've read in the newspaper that the killings on that night were all legally sanctioned, to put down a revolt against the government."

"I assure you Frau—"

"Frau Teeling. Pastor Wilhelm would never have been involved in anything like that. He dedicated his life to helping others. He had no interest in politics." She sniffed loudly and reached for a handkerchief in her sleeve. "He was a wonderful man. He worked tirelessly with young men who had fallen from grace, to steer them onto the path of righteousness."

"I assure you, Frau Teeling, there is no suggestion that the pastor was involved in the attempted coup."

She brightened, attempting a smile. "You mean he died of natural causes? His heart was not strong, you know."

"You said he worked with young men. Was that in the Graf Spee boxing club?"

"Yes, there and in other clubs around the city. I warned him that he was working too hard. I told him he was risking his health."

"The pastor was murdered," said Keller bluntly.

Saxon frowned at him. Frau Teeling burst into tears.

They had to wait several minutes before she was calm enough to answer more questions.

Keller asked her, "Do you live here, Frau Teeling?"

"No, my own lodgings are a few streets away."

"So the pastor was alone in this house the night he died?"

"Yes. I found his body the next morning. He was lying in the hallway."

Saxon said, "Have you any idea who might have wanted him dead? Did he have any enemies?"

She wailed again. "No. He had no enemies. Pastor Wilhelm was a walking saint. Everybody loved the man."

#

Back at the station, Saxon placed the professor's report on the dead boy into his file. The second report he put into a new manila file and marked it 'Pastor Wilhelm Berger.'

A quick glance at Bernhard Franck's picture confirmed what Keller had said. Bernhard Franck, showing the effects of a hard life, was now the doorman at the nightclub. He had been a good-looking man in his youth.

Two hours of diligent work by Keller on the station records confirmed what Saxon had suspected: Fingerprints collected from the burglaries matched those of Stephan Weiss, Johann Grau and Lottie Kleiner – taken from the glass tumbler.

"It makes sense, Boss," said Keller. "They were all small people, ideal for squeezing through small spaces. But who were they working for? They can't have been working on their own."

It was eight o'clock by that time. Saxon sent a uniformed officer out to a delicatessen to get them a quick meal.

Glasser slithered into Saxon's office. "You've made some progress, I hear."

"The professor says that Grau was murdered. And we've established that he and Stephan Weiss were involved in a number of our burglary cases, along with Lottie Kleiner."

Glasser shook his head. "I can't believe that delightful creature could be mixed up in anything so sordid as burglary."

"We'll know soon enough," said Saxon. "We are just about to pick her up again. With any luck she'll tell us who killed the two boys."

Keller went to the car pool to get a car. Glasser returned to his office. Saxon loaded his handgun and slipped it into his holster.

Glasser reappeared with his tunic buttoned. He spotted the new file on Saxon's desk. "Why the new file? I thought we agreed the pastor died of natural causes?"

"The Medical Examiner tells us the good pastor's heart failed when someone attempted to strangle him."

"So he was murdered? Do you have any suspects?"

"None."

Keller arrived rattling a set of car keys, and Glasser followed Saxon through the door. Keller took the wheel. Glasser sat in the front passenger seat and Saxon sat in the back, feeling like a minor character in his own investigation.

#

The apartment block was guarded by a stern-looking janitor. Once again, Glasser used his Kripo disk to gain entry. They knocked on Lottie's apartment door. No one answered.

"Open it," said Glasser.

The janitor searched his bundle of keys for the right one. After two unsuccessful tries, Glasser said, "Break it down, Keller."

Keller took a step back, but before he could put his boot through the door, Saxon tried the handle. The door swung open. They stepped inside.

Saxon had seen what burglars had done to dozens of homes, but he'd never seen anything like this. The whole place had been ransacked.

There was debris everywhere. Steeling himself for what they might find, he drew his gun.

They searched the apartment, but the intruder was gone, and they found no sign of the girl, alive or dead.

"Thank God." Glasser shuddered. "I was sure we were going to find her in the bedroom or the bathroom."

Saxon asked the janitor how such a thing could have happened. Had he let any strangers into the building in the last few days?

"No, no one."

Hadn't he heard anything? Whoever did this must have made a lot of noise.

The janitor gave an indifferent shrug. "I'm not on guard 24 hours of every day. I have to eat. I have to buy food. A determined criminal could easily get inside."

Saxon examined the apartment door. It had been broken open.

Keller looked around in disgust. "Another burglary for our files, Boss."

"This was no burglary," said Saxon. "Whoever did this was searching for something."

"Who were they, Boss, and what were they searching for?"

"And what have they done with the lovely Lottie?" said Glasser.

#

They crammed into the car again.

This time, Glasser took the back seat. "Is it far?" he said.

"The north side of the city, sir. We should be there in thirty minutes."

"Use your, bell, man. Get us there in fifteen."

Keller put the bell on and they raced across the city.

At the door to the nightclub, Glasser flashed his Kripo disk. Bernhard the doorman stood aside to let them in. They stood near the bar while their eyes adjusted to the gloom. The same waitress as before appeared and asked what they would like to drink.

"Nothing," said Glasser. "We're here to speak with Lottie Kleiner."

The waitress smiled at Glasser. "If you stand at the bar you must order a drink, sir."

Glasser flashed his Kripo disk at her. "Is Lottie Kleiner here?"

"I don't think she's in tonight, sir. I'll check." She scuttled away.

Glasser ran his eyes over the men at the bar and the dancers. "What kind of club is this?"

The man behind the bar responded, "It's a men's club. Can I get you something to drink?"

"We're looking for Lottie Kleiner. Is she in the club?" said Saxon.

"Lottie's not here tonight. You should talk to her boyfriend, Hermann. He's over there." He nodded toward a table occupied by two young men.

Glasser led the way to the table.

"Which one of you is Hermann?" he said.

One of the young men got up and disappeared into the crowd. The second man peered at them. "I'm Hermann."

All three policemen sat at the table with Hermann.

"We're looking for Lottie Kleiner," said Glasser. "You are her boyfriend?"

Hermann smiled and a strange sense of déjà vu ran down Saxon's spine. "You could say that. Why do you ask?"

Glasser flashed his Kripo disk again. "We have some questions for her. Where can we find her?"

"She's at home. I can give you the address."

"We've been there," said Keller. "Where else could she be?"

Hermann shrugged.

#

Back at base, Glasser said, "Degenerates will do just as well as Jews for quota purposes. We will raid that club and arrest everyone. But do nothing until I've spoken to my contact in the newspapers. *Beobachter* will certainly take it and *Der Stürmer* may be interested."

Saxon was horrified by the prospect of a raid on the club. Everyone arrested would be sent to the labour camps. He pointed out that Glasser had been seen entering the club.

Glasser fixed Saxon with his pin eyes. "What's your point?"

"It might be suggested that you are one of them. You know how mud sticks."

Glasser grunted. "Speaking to undesirables is part of my job."

"Indeed," said Saxon.

"You never married, did you, sir?" said Keller.

"That's insubordination. What are you implying?"

"I'm implying nothing, sir. But you know what the newspapers are like. It's all a matter of appearances."

Chapter 6

Early Tuesday morning, Lottie called Keller on the telephone. She was in tears. "My apartment has been destroyed."

"We saw that last night. We were looking for you. Where were you?"

"I was with friends. What can I do, Kommissar?"

Keller said nothing to correct her mistake. 'Kommissar Keller' had a certain ring to it. "Do you have somewhere to stay?"

"One of my friends will make room for me. But I don't feel safe. I'm sure this has something to do with the deaths of Johann and Stephan. What if I'm next?"

"Come into the station after nine this morning. We'll see what needs to be done."

When Lottie arrived at the station, Keller took her straight into Saxon's office. She was wearing a white shirt and dark pants that gave her a slightly dominant look that Saxon found appealing. He gave her a cigarette. Keller lit it for her. She crossed her legs.

She had been crying. Her eye makeup was smudged, her eyes red-rimmed, and Saxon noticed a tremor in her hands.

He said, "You told Keller that you thought there might be a connection between the destruction to your apartment and the deaths of the two boys, Johann Grau and Stephan Weiss. Can you tell me why?"

She shrugged. "We three were close. We did everything together."

"Including burglaries?" She opened her mouth to object, but he held up a hand to stop her. "No point in denying it, Fräulein, we have found all three sets of fingerprints at the scenes of several burglaries. Would you like to tell us who you were working for?"

Her lips closed in a tight line. She leaned forward to tap ash from her cigarette into Saxon's ashtray.

Keller said, "Was it your boyfriend, Hermann?"

"No, no, Hermann had nothing to do with it."

"Who, then?" said Saxon.

She took a moment before stubbing her cigarette out in the ashtray. "I don't deny it, Kommissar. We were led astray by an older man that we all admired."

"The name of this older man?"

She gave no answer.

"We know it was Fritz Franck, the boxing coach," said Saxon.

She blushed. "You must understand we only did it to please him."

"Not for the money?" said Keller.

Saxon spoke quietly. "Tell me how that worked."

"He told us which houses were empty. We would get in wherever we could. We stole jewellery and small ornaments. Anything that might be valuable."

Saxon offered her another cigarette. She took one, and Keller lit it again. "He gave us very little money. Enough for cigarettes and an occasional glass of wine."

Saxon said, "Tell me why you think the murders of the two boys might be connected to these burglaries."

"I didn't say that, Kommissar. Johann, Stephan and I were very close. They were both murdered. When my apartment was searched, I thought—"

"Searched? Your apartment was searched? What do you think they were searching for?"

"I'm sorry, I have no idea."

Keller said, "Did they take anything?"

"It's impossible to say. You saw the place. Everything was destroyed."

Saxon said, "You will be charged with breaking into people's houses and theft. You will be held here until we have apprehended Franck."

Keller called a uniformed patrolman who escorted Lottie to the cells.

#

They drove to the boxing club. The old janitor barred their way, but they pushed past him without ceremony.

"There he goes!" Keller shouted.

Saxon caught a glimpse of a stocky figure sprinting through a door at the back of the gym. Keller gave chase. Saxon left through the front door, circled around toward the back, and came face to face with Fritz Franck in a narrow passage at the side of the building.

Kommissar Saxon held up a palm. "Give yourself up, Franck. There's nowhere you can go, nowhere you can hide."

Franck's eyes narrowed. He pulled out a knife and waved it at Saxon. "Stand aside!"

"Drop the knife, man. I'm a police officer. Use that on me and they'll string you up from the nearest tree."

Franck took a step closer. "I said stand aside, *Bulle*."

Saxon reached inside his jacket for his gun, but before he could draw it, Franck was on him. They crashed to the ground together. Saxon was no match for the stocky boxer. It was all he could do to hold Franck's knife hand at bay.

"Drop the weapon and stand up." The command was accompanied by a loud click.

Keller stood over the boxing coach, the barrel of his gun pressing against the back of his head. Everything froze. The one thought in Saxon's head was that if Keller fired, the bullet would probably pass right through Franck's head and kill both of them.

Franck dropped the knife. Saxon scrambled out from under him, and Keller put Franck in handcuffs.

#

They took the boxing coach back to the police station and put him in interview room one. Saxon began the interrogation by accusing him of organizing the burglaries and selling the stolen goods. Franck stubbornly refused to answer. Saxon told him that Dieter Peters had been found in possession of a significant amount of the stolen property and had named Franck as his supplier. Franck said nothing.

Saxon told him that he had a confession from one of the people who carried out the burglaries. They had named him as the organizer. Franck snorted.

"Nothing to say?"

Franck crossed his arms high on his chest.

"In that case, Fritz Franck, I am charging you with the double murder of two of your accomplices, Stephan Weiss and Johann Grau."

Franck jumped to his feet. "God in heaven! I never killed anybody."

"I think you did."

"Why would I kill my team?"

"So you admit the boys carried out the burglaries for you?"

"Yes, yes, the boys helped with the jobs, but you can't put their killings on my shoulders."

"You paid them for what they stole?"

"I paid them to do the jobs."

"How much?"

"A few Marks."

Keller said, "We found 3,000 Marks in Johann Grau's house."

Franck's wide-eyed amazement looked genuine. "I never paid him anything like that."

"Then who did? And who do think might have killed them?" said Saxon.

"And why?" said Keller.

#

It was dark by the time they'd finished interrogating the boxing coach. They charged him with multiple counts of burglary and locked him in a cell. They charged Lottie with the minor offence of aiding in the execution of the burglaries.

"I'm letting you go, under license," said Saxon. "Do you have somewhere safe to spend the night?"

"I think so."

"We'd like to see you again in the morning. Can I rely on you to come back in?"

She batted her eyelashes. "Yes, of course, Kommissar."

He put on his stern face. "I want to see you here at nine o'clock. If you make us come and find you, the charges will be more severe."

"I understand."

When she'd gone, Keller fetched two cups of coffee and a couple of apple pastries. Saxon and Keller settled down in Saxon's office to discuss the case.

Saxon lit a cigarette. "We must assume that the money in Grau's possession and the cash that paid for Herr Weiss's automobile didn't come from the boys' burgling activities. They must have had another source of funds."

"Blackmail, perhaps?" said Keller.

"My thought exactly," said Saxon. "The boys shared many activities. The burglaries, the boxing, and probably the nightclub, as well. That place is a den of iniquity. Herr Weiss blamed the people there for corrupting his boy."

"He could be right, Boss."

"That seems likely. Let us assume that the boys were engaged in unnatural practices with some pervert from the nightclub..."

"And they decided to blackmail whoever that was."

"Yes. I think Lottie was involved somehow. Whatever proof the boys had – photographs, probably – we must assume the pervert was searching for that in Lottie's apartment."

"The three of them were close, Boss. Lottie said that. And we know they were all involved in Franck's burglaries. Do you think Lottie's boyfriend was involved too?"

"More than likely. He was certainly small and slim enough for the work." Saxon stood and began prowling around the office. "Whoever killed Stephan Weiss must be a member of the SS. He had prior knowledge of what was going to happen on the night of June 30, and he hoped the killing would be lost among the general carnage."

"Fritz Franck is a member of the SS, Boss."

"Yes, and so is the rich philanthrope, Emil Richter."

"How does the pastor's death fit into all this, Boss?"

"Heaven knows, Keller. It's difficult to see a connection."

They called it a night, and Saxon made his way home.

#

Once again, Ruth was juggling a crying baby with one arm while preparing a bottle for him with the other. Saxon took the baby from her.

She smiled at him. "Samuel said his first big word. He said 'giraffe.'"

Saxon held the infant in front of him. "Did you, little man? Did you say a big word like that?"

Samuel gurgled.

Ruth picked up the toy giraffe and handed it to Samuel. "What is this? Samuel? What do you call this?"

Samuel blew bubbles.

"Giraffe. Say it for your papa, Samuel. Say giraffe. Gi-raffe."

Samuel smiled and broke wind.

"He really did say it. I know you don't believe me."

"I believe you, Ruth. Give him time, I'm sure he'll say it again."

Ruth took the baby back and he burst into tears. She shook her head. "He really loves his papa." She put the bottle in his mouth, and Samuel stopped screaming.

Lying in bed that night, Saxon listened to Ruth's rhythmical breathing beside him. He recalled what Ruth had said about Samuel. He was like two people in one body, screaming in his mother's arms, but quiet in his father's.

Saxon sat bolt upright in the bed.

That was why Lottie had never been in the BDM, and why they had never seen Hermann and Lottie in the same place together. Lottie and Hermann were one and the same person! Whatever unnatural practices the boys had been up to, Hermann must have been involved as well. Hermann could be in mortal danger.

He slipped from the bed and put his clothes on. He left the apartment as quietly as he could and found a taxi to take him to the Black Flamingo nightclub.

The doorman made no attempt to prevent him from entering. He went straight to the bar and asked the bartender if Hermann or Lottie were in the club.

"I haven't seen either of them," said the barman.

Saxon ran back up the stairs to the street and hailed a passing taxi. "Take me to the Graf Spee boxing club."

"It's not far," said the driver. "You could walk there in ten minutes."

Saxon flashed his Kripo badge. "Take me there."

The boxing club was locked up for the night. Saxon ran his eyes over the building from the opposite side of the road and caught a fleeting glimpse of a light upstairs in a third-floor window.

He ran to the back of the building, used the butt of his gun to smash a small pane of glass, reached in and opened the door. Moonlight flooding through the windows helped him to find a staircase at the rear of the gym. Gun in hand, he ran up the stairs.

He reached the third floor and took a moment to get his bearings. Then he heard a sound and moved toward it. He was in a dark corridor with doors leading to rooms left and right. He carried on down the corridor, ears tuned to pick up the slightest sounds.

When the sound came, it was not what he expected, a scream of pain and anguish, the like of which he had never heard before, coming from one of the rooms he'd already passed. He drew his gun, moved back to the door, turned the handle and flung it open.

Chapter 7

Weak moonlight from the window lit the figure of Hermann, strapped to a chair in the middle of a room. He was nearly naked, blood trailing from his nose and the corner of his eyes.

Emil Richter stood over him, wearing a single boxing glove.

Saxon levelled his handgun at the big man. "Leave him, Richter. Drop the glove."

Richter stepped back. The glove hit the bare floorboards with a clunk. It was weighted. "This is not what it seems, Kommissar."

"Face the wall. Put your hands behind your back." Saxon reached for his handcuffs. "I'm arresting you for serious assault."

Richter stood facing the wall. "This is nothing but a piece of theatrical foreplay. You've heard of the Marquis de Sade?"

Saxon secured his prisoner with the handcuffs. "Explain it to the judge."

He bent down to free Hermann from his restraints. "Are you all right?"

Hermann spoke in a strangled voice. "Thank God you found me. He killed Stephan and Johann. He would have killed me, too. Behind you, Kommissar!"

Saxon straightened his back, drawing his gun.

Too late.

The point of a knife broke the skin under Saxon's chin. "Drop the gun, *Bulle*, or I'll slit your throat where you stand."

Saxon recognized the voice and foul breath of Bernhard Franck, the doorman from the nightclub, the boxing coach's brother. He dropped his gun. It clattered onto the floorboards.

Bernhard placed a hand on Saxon's back and pushed him forward. "Now you face the wall."

Saxon stood beside Richter, facing the wall. "You're only making matters worse for both of you, Bernhard. Put the knife down and let me do my job."

Bernhard picked up the gun. He searched Saxon's pockets, removed the keys to the handcuffs and freed Richter.

Richter secured Saxon's hands with his own handcuffs. "Good boy, Bernhard," he said.

"This is madness, Richter," said Saxon. "Assaulting the boy is bad enough but interfering with a police officer is much more serious."

Richter turned to his companion in crime. "Shoot him. Shoot the *Bulle*, Bernhard."

The doorman made no move to comply. Wearing his trilby, he stood with his arms by his sides, the gun in one hand, the knife in the other. His broken nose looked grotesque in the shadowy moonlight.

"What's on your mind, now? Shoot him. He has seen too much. We have to get rid of him."

Bernhard's face contorted, as if wrestling with conflicting thoughts. "I – I don't think..."

"What? Haven't I told you before? Leave the thinking to me. Now do what I ask. Then you can help me get what I need from pretty boy, here."

The doorman stepped toward Saxon. "I'm sorry," he said, pointing the gun at Saxon's chest.

Facing the barrel of his own gun, Saxon's mouth dried. "Don't do this, Bernhard. You're not a murderer."

Bernhard cocked the gun. Then he swivelled on his heel and fired.

Richter gave a strangled cry and crumpled to the floor, blood pouring from a hole in his chest. Bernhard dropped the gun and fell to his knees, cradling Richter's head in his lap.

Tears flowed down Bernhard's face. "I'm sorry, Emil. Please forgive me. You know I love you. I've always loved you."

Richter gurgled once, and the light of life left his eyes.

"Take off these handcuffs," said Saxon.

He got no response.

"Can you hear me, Franck? Set me free."

Hermann said, "Remove the handcuffs, Bernhard. It's over."

#

Hermann went to a bathroom to tidy up his face. When he returned, he was transformed into the voluptuous Lottie, dressed in a shiny, tight-fitting blue dress, the blond wig flowing across her shoulders, stunning as ever, despite the facial bruising.

Saxon used the telephone in the club office to call Keller. Keller arrived in a car within 30 minutes. As they emerged from the boxing club, blood-red skies over Munich welcomed them with a glorious summer sunrise.

Back at the station, they interviewed Bernhard Franck first, but got nothing from him. His mind was gone. All he would say was, "I used to be his pretty boy," over and over.

Lottie told them the whole sordid story. Richter was a sexual deviant with a preference for young men and teenage boys. He liked to dress up, and he encouraged the boys to do the same.

Three of his victims, Johann, Stephan and Hermann had got together and used a hidden camera to take incriminating photographs of the perverted philanthrope. They demanded money for their silence, and Richter had paid them in exchange for the pictures and the negatives.

The boys held back some of the pictures, but when they tried to visit the well a second time, Richter turned on them, resorting to burglary in search of the photographs, and eventually, to murder.

Keller filled in the rest. "He killed Johann Grau first, threw him in the lake, weighed down with rocks. The boy should never have resurfaced from his watery grave. Then he shot Stephan Weiss. As a member of the SS, Richter would have had advance knowledge of the Führer's plans for the Night of the Long Knives. He chose that night in to make it easier to cover up his crime."

"I assume that Richter never found the rest of the incriminating pictures," said Saxon. "Is that why he was beating you?"

Lottie sniffed, her fingers playing with a strand of her hair. "Yes, but I don't have the pictures. I'm sure he would have killed me if you hadn't come to the rescue and Bernhard hadn't turned on Richter the way he did."

"So where are the photographs?" said Keller.

"Stephan had them. I thought Richter must have recovered them when Stephan died."

Word of Lottie's rescue had reached Glasser, and he joined Saxon and Keller in the interview room. He gushed at Lottie, grabbing her hand. "I'm so pleased you weren't seriously injured, my dear. It pains me to think of the way that brute, Richter, beat you. How are you feeling now?"

"Show him, Lottie," said Saxon, to spare Glasser any more embarrassment.

Lottie removed her wig. She pulled down the front of her dress, exposing a pair of rubber breasts.

"Meet Hermann," said Saxon.

The blood drained from Glasser's face.

Keller stood facing the wall with a hand clamped over his mouth. Glasser left the room without a word. Once he was outside, Keller and Saxon burst into raucous laughter. Hermann joined in.

Saxon asked Hermann about the pastor. "Was he involved in these deviant activities?

"Oh no," said Hermann. "Pastor Berger was a saint. He did what he could for us boys."

#

"So who killed the pastor?" said Keller, after Lottie/Hermann had gone.

Saxon lit a cigarette and took a long drag. "Whoever it was hated him enough to try and strangle him to death in his own house."

"I think Richter killed the pastor, Boss."

"Why would he? The pastor brought a patina of respectability to the boxing club."

"Suppose the pastor stumbled across the perversions and had to be silenced."

Saxon shook his head. "Weiss would be my guess. Remember what he said. He said the degenerate sodomites from the club corrupted his son. What if he was talking about the boxing club, not the nightclub?"

"That sounds like he knew what was going on, Boss, but why kill the pastor? The pastor had nothing to do with any of the perversions."

"Those missing photographs are the key to everything, Keller. We need to locate them. Get us a car."

While Keller ran to the car pool, Saxon slipped out and bought a copy of the *Völkischer Beobachter* newspaper. Richter's picture dominated the front page. The inside pages had pictures of the boxing club and the story of the philanthrope's deviant practices with the boys. Saxon guessed the boxing club janitor must have spilled the beans.

#

The Herr Weiss who opened the door was a pale shadow of the man they'd met before. They followed him into the parlour, where the morning edition of *Völkischer Beobachter* lay scattered on the floor.

"Have you seen what they're saying about my son?"

Keller said, "Are you denying it?"

Weiss shook his head. "How can I deny it? I know what Stephan did. He was young and impressionable."

Saxon said, "You knew what Stephan and his friends were doing with Emil Richter?"

"I worked it out."

Saxon nodded. "And you knew the boys were extorting money from Richter."

"What? No. Who told you that?"

Saxon held out a hand. "Give me the photographs."

"I don't have any photographs."

Keller said, "Is that your Horch V8 outside?"

"Yes, it's mine."

Saxon said, "Where did you get the money to buy that, Herr Weiss?"

"I earned it."

"Working as a labourer on the railways?"

"I saved the money over several years. What are you suggesting, Kommissar?"

Saxon lit a cigarette. "I'm suggesting that you extorted a lot of money from Richter and used it to buy that car."

Weiss's rising panic was visible on his mousey face. "I knew nothing about it until... afterwards."

Keller said, "Since the Enabling Act, blackmail is a capital offense, Herr Weiss. Give us the pictures or we'll have to charge you."

"I don't have them, I swear."

Saxon said, "We can get a warrant to search the house if we have to. Empty your pockets."

"All right, all right." Weiss opened his jacket, pulled out an envelope, and handed it to Saxon.

Saxon emptied the envelope onto the table. There were three photographs. One showed Richter engaged in a lewd act with Johann Grau, dressed as a nurse. The other two showed Richter with Stephan Weiss. Richter was wearing a clerical gown. Stephan was dressed as a fireman, complete with brass helmet. In all of the pictures, Richter's face was obscured.

Keller said, "Richter's face is not clear in these pictures, Boss."

Saxon tossed his cigarette into the fireplace. "So tell us why you murdered Pastor Wilhelm Berger, Herr Weiss."

"I killed no one, I swear, Kommissar."

"You found these photographs, saw a large man in clerical garb, and you thought the pastor was corrupting your son. Is that why you killed him?"

"I swear it wasn't me."

"Who, then?" said Saxon.

"I showed the photographs to Tristan Grau."

They put Weiss in handcuffs and placed him in the car. Then they drove to the Grau home.

Keller hammered on the door. Frau Grau opened it. She had been crying again. She told Keller that her husband had gone to work in the town hall.

The 12 noon Glockenspiel display was just starting when they arrived in Marienplatz. The square was crowded with tourists, all craning their necks and pointing upward.

Saxon assumed they were watching the musical display until he looked up and saw Tristan Grau sitting on a third-floor window ledge.

Saxon and Keller ran up the stairs to the third floor, and quickly located the right room. Saxon approached Grau, now standing on the window ledge.

"Don't do this, Tristan. Think of your poor wife. She's lost a son. You can't inflict any more grief on her."

"Don't try to stop me," said Grau, "I have no choice. I have committed a grievous sin against God."

"Pastor Berger was an old man. He had a weak heart."

"I know. And my action hastened his death."

Saxon took a couple of steps closer. "Why did you attack him?"

"Stay back, Kommissar. I was angry. When I saw those pictures, I thought he was the one who corrupted Stephan. But I was wrong. I killed the wrong man."

Out of the corner of his eye, Saxon saw Keller circling toward Grau.

Saxon moved to his left to distract Grau from Keller. "You made a mistake, Tristan. I'm sure God will forgive you, but not if you take your own life."

Keller lunged toward Grau, wrapping his arms around his legs.

"I have him, Boss—" And Grau vanished.

The cries of horror from the tourists in the square below coincided with the triple cockcrow signalling the end of the Glockenspiel noonday display.

#

Glasser demanded that they charge Weiss with murder.

"I have no evidence that he killed anyone," said Saxon.

"Well, charge him with something. I have to have something to report to Gestapo *Hauptamt*."

"You can tell them that Richter killed the two boys and Grau killed the pastor. Surely, two dead murderers is a fine result. It saves the Fatherland the cost of two expensive trials."

"There is that, I suppose. And we can charge Bernhard Franck with Richter's death."

"We can, but no one would blame him, given Richter's heinous crimes. And besides, Franck is unfit to stand trial. But you can add both Franck brothers to your quota of undesirables."

Glasser shook his head. "You can forget about the quota. I've decided not to put my name forward for the Schutzstaffel training school."

Saxon was relieved. Ruth and Samuel were no longer at immediate risk.

#

Bouncing Samuel on his knee that evening, Saxon tried to imagine what he would do if he discovered that his own son had been corrupted by an older man.

"Papa," said Samuel, handing his giraffe to his father.

Saxon smiled at him. "Thank you, Samuel."

Assuming he was certain who the defiler was, would he kill him? Yes, he would. Would he be prepared to hang to rid the world of a child molester?

"Giraffe," said Samuel, clear as a bell.

No question about it.

THE END

Thanks for reading this story. If you liked it, tell your friends. If you want to encourage the author to write more like this, please write a review. Reviews really help.

ABOUT THE AUTHOR

JJ Toner writes short stories and thrillers. He lives in Ireland with his wife and youngest child. https://www.JJToner.com/

Check out the first Saxon short story
ZUGZWANG